I HAVE TWO FAMILIES

I Have Two Families

Doris Wild Helmering
Illustrated by Heidi Palmer

Abingdon
Nashville

I Have Two Families

Copyright © 1981 by Doris Wild Helmering
All Rights Reserved

Library of Congress Cataloging in Publication Data
Helmering, Doris Wild, 1942-
 I have two families.
 SUMMARY: Patty describes her feelings about her parents'
divorce and the living arrangements they decided upon.
 [1. Divorce—Fiction] I. Title.
PZ7.H3758Iah   [E]   80-22392

ISBN 0-687-18507-6

Manufactured in the United States of America

To Germaine

CHAPTER 1

Hi. I'm Patty and I'm eight years old. I live at 1622A Skinker Avenue. I have a friend and her name is Jane. When my friend Jane gets mad at me, she tells everyone that I live on Stinker Avenue. I also live at 22C Park Street. You see, Mom and Dad are divorced; so, I have two families.

I live with Dad and my brother, Michael, and Pancake, my dog, at 1622A Skinker Avenue, and I live with Mom and Michael, and our cat, Harry, at 22C Park Street.

Lots of kids at school think that when your Mom and Dad get a divorce it's real bad. At first I thought it was real bad, too—especially when I knew that my parents were getting a divorce, and I didn't know what was going to happen to me. That's the scary part, not knowing what's going to happen.

I used to go to bed at night and wonder if I would live with Dad or with Mom. Maybe Dad would take Michael to live with him because Michael's a boy. And Mom would take me because I'm a girl. That way we would all have somebody to live with and nobody would get lonesome.

One day after school I told Jane, my best friend, what I thought was going to happen—me with Mom and Michael with Dad.

Jane thought that this was a good idea! No more Michael to bug Jane and me when we wanted to talk. No more sharing with Michael or picking up his messes! In other words, no more pesty brother! Maybe this divorce thing wouldn't be too bad after all.

Funny thing though, when I went home from Jane's house, I started thinking about not living with Michael.

It's true that Michael is a pest. No doubt about it. But Michael is also my brother. And you are supposed to live with your brother.

Well, my parents were just going to have to come up with another plan for us, because Michael and me were going to live together!

One day I decided to ask Michael what he thought was going to happen to us. Michael was coloring. At first Michael wouldn't talk to me. He just sort of acted like I wasn't there. When he did talk to me, his voice sounded, well, sort of scared. What he told me was that he thought nobody would want to live with him.

I put my hand on Michael's shoulder and told Michael I would want to live with him. Michael didn't answer me, but I know he felt better.

I did notice that after our talk Michael started putting away his toys and cleaning up his messes. He even helped with the dishes one time. I guess Michael was trying to be nice, so Mom or Dad would want to live with him.

I really felt sorry for Michael. If you ask me, divorce stinks!

My Mom and Dad used to love each other, and they wanted to live together. They used to tell us stories about how they met and fell in love.

Then all of a sudden they didn't want to live together. I kept thinking what if Mom and Dad would fall out of love with me? What if they didn't want to live with me?

CHAPTER 2

One day Dad and Mom called us into the living room for a talk. I knew that it was going to be a serious talk. I started getting butterflies in my stomach . . . like when the teacher calls on me and I don't know the answer.

Michael looked like he was going to cry. He was scared. Mom looked like she was going to cry. So did Dad. In fact, the only one who didn't look sad was Pancake. He kept playing with his rag doll on the floor.

Mom cleared her throat. She always does that when she wants to get our attention. She said that although she and Dad had decided not to live together, she and Dad still loved Michael and me very much. And she and Dad were very concerned about our welfare. (I guess that meant they were worried about where we were going to live and who we were going to live with.)

Mom said that because Dad has a job with very regular hours they had decided that both of us would live with Dad.

Mom has funny hours. She works for an airline and makes reservations for people. Sometimes she works during the day and sometimes she works at night. So it would really be hard for her to take care of us.

Mom said that we would work out a schedule so we could be with her, too. But mainly we would live with Dad.

Boy, did I feel better. Michael and I were both picked. And we didn't even have to choose between Mom or Dad.

Jane, my friend, said that sometimes children have to decide which parent they want to live with. I sure didn't want to do that. I just couldn't choose. You see, even though my parents are divorced, I love them very much.

So, that's how it happened that I have two families. I live with Dad and Michael and Pancake, our dog, at Skinker Avenue most of the time, and I live with Mom and Michael and Harry, our cat, at Park Street part of the time.

CHAPTER 3

Want to know what I do at 1622A Skinker Avenue? Well, first thing in the morning Dad wakes us up. I used to wake up with an alarm clock, but my clock is broken, so Dad has to wake me up.

I don't much like getting up in the morning. But I have to do it. Like Dad says, "We've all got to cooperate so everyone gets where they are going on time." Sometimes Michael tells Dad that he doesn't mind cooperating but he does mind getting up.

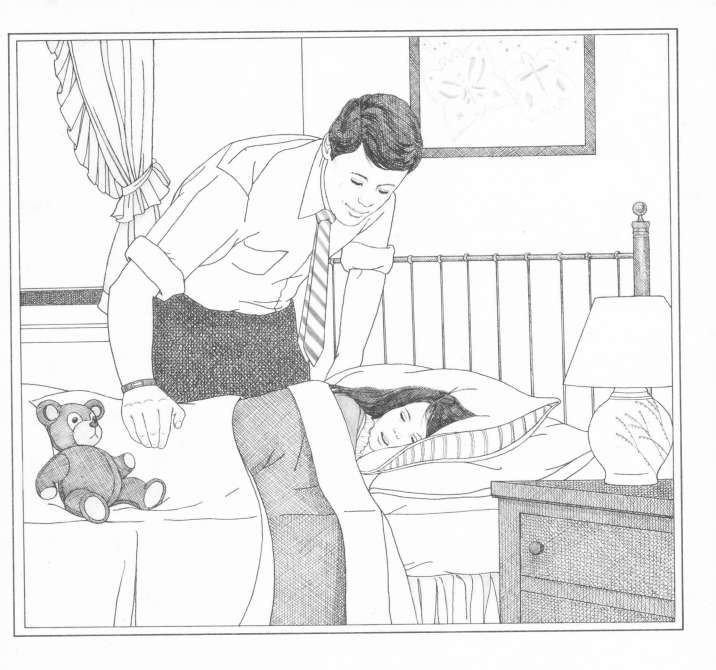

After I get dressed, we have breakfast. Sometimes we have cereal, sometimes eggs, and sometimes pancakes. Mostly, though, we have cereal. When breakfast is finished, Dad and I clear off the table. If we don't have enough time, we don't get the table cleared off, and the mess has to stay all day. Dad doesn't like it when this happens.

When it's time to leave the house, Dad calls, "Train leaves in five minutes. All aboard." That means we had better hurry. Of course, we don't ride a train, but we do ride the elevator to the basement to get our car.

Sometimes after we get to the basement, we have to ride the elevator up again because I forgot my lunch or Michael forgot his coat. That's when our family at Skinker Avenue doesn't get along very well. Dad gets mad because he is going to be late for work. I get mad because I'm going to be late for school. And we get scared because Dad hollers.

Michael goes to day care, and he doesn't have to be there at any special time. Lucky Michael!

Lately, Dad has been laying out Michael's clothes, including his coat, so Michael won't forget anything. I also put my books and coat by the door. Dad puts his briefcase and umbrella and coat by the door. Dad says, "We've got to have a system."

I like my Dad a lot.

The car ride takes about a half hour. Michael is dropped off at day care, I get dropped off at school, then Dad goes to work. Good thing Pancake doesn't need to be dropped off somewhere.

After school I walk to Jane's house. She's my friend who teases me about living on Stinker instead of Skinker. When we get to Jane's house, we usually have a snack, and then we roller-skate or ride bikes. Sometimes we just sit and talk.

Dad picks me up from Jane's house at about 5:30. He already has Michael in the car. On the way home we play a game called "Catch-up."

Dad catches us up on what he did during the day. Then Michael tells us what happened at day care. Then I tell what happened at school. The rule of the game is that you have to share at least two things. Dad says that this game teaches people to share. This is one of my favorite times during the day.

When we get home, it is my job to feed Pancake and set

the table. Dad looks at the mail and then makes dinner. He makes hamburger, fried potatoes with onions, peas, and salad. Sometimes he cooks eggs and sausage. Sometimes we have chili. Michael sits at the table and watches us get dinner ready. Sometimes Michael gets the napkins out for me.

In the evening Michael and I play Chinese checkers, watch television, or read books. Sometimes we help Dad do the dishes. He reads the paper, pays bills, and sometimes has to sew a button on one of our coats. Dad is very busy. At 8:30 we go to bed.

CHAPTER 4

On Wednesday Mom picks up Michael from day care and me from school. I don't go to Jane's house on Wednesday. Then we go to our apartment on Park Street. At 22C Park Street, I have to clean out the dishwasher and help Mom get dinner. Michael has to feed Harry, our cat, and set the table.

Sometimes Michael fusses because at Skinker Avenue he doesn't have to set the table. Mom laughs and gives him a love tap on his bottom. Then she says, "Every family is different, you know."

After dinner, we play cards. Sometimes we watch television together, and sometimes Mom reads to us. She just finished reading us *Pinocchio.*

When Mom is too tired to read or play with us, she reads her paper or talks on the telephone. I don't like it when she talks on the telephone.

We go to bed on Park Street at the same time we go to bed on Skinker Avenue. So . . . sometimes my two families are the same.

On Thursday morning, I get up and dress. My alarm clock on Park Street works. Then we have breakfast. We eat oatmeal, hot cocoa, and cinnamon toast.

After breakfast we make our beds while Mom cleans the kitchen. Then Mom braids my hair. My friends at school always know when I stay with Mom because of the braids.

Mom drives Michael to day care and me to school. If Mom doesn't have to go to work that day, she drives me to school. Then Michael doesn't go to day care. Mom and Michael get to spend the day together. Sometimes I wish I was little again so I could spend the day with Mom.

Thursday nights we go back to Skinker Avenue with Dad and Pancake.

CHAPTER 5

Our weekends are spent mostly with Dad. On Saturdays, Michael and I get to sleep late. Dad says, "Children need their rest." Dad sleeps late, too, so I say, "Dad needs his rest."

When we get up, we eat, get dressed, clean the apartment, and then we go to the supermarket.

My job at the supermarket is to get the apples, bananas, potatoes, lettuce, eggs, cheese, butter, and cereal. Michael gets the milk, juice, and bread. Dad takes care of the rest.

When we get to the store, Dad says, "Off you go." Each of us gets a cart and off we go. Then we meet at the checkout counter and put everything in one cart so the cashier can ring us out.

Shopping is fun and makes us feel like grown-ups.

On Saturday afternoon we go roller-skating or to the movies. The first Saturday of every month all of us go out for lunch.

Every once in a while somebody at school asks me how it is when your parents are divorced. I tell them that sometimes it's a pain. Like when you want to ride your bicycle and your bicycle is at your other house. Or you want to wear your red jacket and it's at the other house. That happened to Michael one time.

Mostly though, I tell the kids that it's okay. I have two beds, two telephones, two alarm clocks (one that works and one that's broken), two addresses, and two families that love me very much. I have Dad, Michael, and Pancake at 1622A Skinker Avenue, and I have Mom, Michael, and Harry at 22C Park Street.

On Sundays we go to Sunday school and then Mom picks us up. We always spend Sundays with Mom. Sometimes we go to a movie, sometimes we go bowling, and sometimes we visit relatives. What I like best though is when we go to Park Street and talk and cook. I know how to make pizza, meat loaf, baked potatoes, salad, and brownies. Michael is a good brownie maker, too. Mom thinks cooking is important for us to know.

Some Sundays we get to stay overnight with Mom. Other times we go back to our other house because of Mom's schedule.

I guess our weekends are pretty normal. It's just that we spend part of them at Park Street and part of them at Skinker Avenue.

One time all of us went to the zoo. It was interesting seeing all the animals. But mostly I was watching how Dad and Laurie acted. Almost the whole time they held hands, and once Dad kissed Laurie. I didn't mind him holding her hand, but kissing, I didn't like that.

Funny though, after we went to the zoo, I liked Laurie better. I think Michael did, too.

Dad didn't say anything that night, but, oh boy, the next day he was really mad at me. He said it was all right not to like it that he was going to date, but I had to be pleasant to the person he was dating. And pleasant means smiling, talking, and especially answering questions.

I know Michael didn't like it either because whenever it was time for Dad to go out with Laurie, Michael got a stomachache. And when Michael feels bad inside, he gets a stomachache.

At first we wouldn't talk to Laurie when she came to the house. I thought that if we didn't talk she would feel bad and go away. I wouldn't even answer her questions.

On Saturday night Dad usually goes out on a date with Laurie. Laurie is a nice person. She doesn't have any children and she is pretty. Of course, she is not as pretty as Mom.

When Dad first started going out, I didn't like it at all. It felt, well, sort of weird. I mean, Dad dating and all.